AUNT FRED
IS A
WITCH

by

Rachna Gilmore

illustrated by

Chum McLeod

SECOND
STORY
Press

To Anne and Alice and Ann, Friday Witches

Canadian Cataloguing in Publication Data

Gilmore, Rachna, 1953-
Aunt Fred is a witch
ISBN 0-929005-23-6
I. McLeod, Chum. II. Title.
PS8563.I57A79 1991   jC813'.54   C91-093881-4
PZ7.G54Au 1991

Printed and bound in Hong Kong
Edited by Peter Carver
Second Story Press gratefully acknowledges
the assistance of the Ontario Arts Council
and the Canada Council

Published by
SECOND STORY PRESS
760 Bathurst St.
Toronto, Canada
M5S 2R6

Aunt Fred's a witch. I know because my cousin Jeremy told me. Jeremy says she works magic, really strange magic, so she's got to be a witch.

So when Mom told me that Aunt Fred had invited me for the weekend, I wasn't thrilled. I'm not afraid of witches. It's just with all that magic stuff you have to be careful around them. Very careful.

I thought about faking sick so I could stay home, but in the end I decided to go. No one in school had ever spent a weekend with a witch. I'd really have something to brag about. Just to be on the safe side, though, I packed a necklace of garlic into my suitcase. Jeremy told me witches hate garlic. It stops them from hexing you.

Mom drove me to Aunt Fred's house, way out in the country. It was surrounded by trees and it was old and tumbledown. Perfect for a witch.

Aunt Fred opened the door. She hugged Mom and smiled at me. At least she didn't try to slobber me with kisses.

I stared at her. She was tiny and wrinkled with eyes like blackcurrants. Her hair was covered with a faded blue scarf and she walked slowly, all hunched over. I couldn't imagine her doing any magic stuff and I felt relieved and annoyed at the same time. Some witch! I wouldn't be telling anyone in school about this weekend.

As soon as Mom had gone Aunt Fred rubbed her hands, laughed and said, "Great! Wait here, Leila, I'm going to change." She straightened up and skipped out of the room.

Change! A chill went down my spine. "This is it," I thought. "This is where she becomes a witch."

I opened my suitcase and whipped out my garlic necklace. I felt a bit silly but I put it on anyway. Just in case.

Soon, I heard Aunt Fred's footsteps running down the stairs. She didn't sound like an old woman.

Aunt Fred breezed into the livingroom. Had she ever changed!

The scarf was gone. Aunt Fred's hair was curly and bright red. She wore a brilliant flowing dress spattered with all the colours of the rainbow. Her face was still wrinkled but her lips were red and her eyelids, green. On her feet were purple sandals, and each toe-nail was painted a different colour.

Aunt Fred raised her arms and swirled around, like a gaudy bird with huge, fluttering wings.

"How d'you like it?" she asked.

I blinked.

"Nice, Aunt Fred," I said, remembering it isn't a good idea to cross a witch. "Real nice."

Aunt Fred grinned. "I thought you'd like it. And Leila, you don't have to call me Aunt Fred. My real name is Winifred Inez Tara Chowdry Hogarth. Just pick one." Her red lips smiled at me. "Or you can call me Witch, for short."

I gulped.

Aunt Fred scrunched up her little black eyes and grabbed my arm.

"Leila! How would you like to be terrified and scream out loud?"

"Scream?" I said in a little voice.

"Yeh! Scream!" Aunt Fred's beady eyes gleamed.

"Well," I squeaked, "I don't want to be picky, but I'm not big on screaming, I'd rather ..."

"There's a fair in town, with some great rides," said Aunt Fred. "Come on, girl, let's go party."

She whipped out two crash-helmets, helped me on to her motorcycle and we were off.

We went on all the fast and crazy rides with loops and spins and dives. Aunt Fred's dress streamed behind, flapping in the wind. I kept expecting her to sail off into the sky, but she held on tight, bouncing and whooping like a little kid. When I yell like that, Mom calls me a bellowing banshee. But we'd come to the fair to scream so I whooped and hollered too.

Of course I kept my garlic necklace on. I knew Aunt Fred was giving me a good time so I'd get careless. If I took my necklace off, she'd hex me.

When we'd finally had enough of the rides Aunt Fred said, "What shall we do now, Leila? Think of something magical, something you've always wanted to do."

"Magical?" I thought. "Not a chance!"

"Let's go roller-skating," I said. I was sure
Aunt Fred would sit down while I skated. That way
I'd be safe from any witch stuff.

But Aunt Fred didn't sit down. Not her. She
whizzed around like she'd been born on wheels. She
took my hand and gave me a spin, yelling "Wheee!"
We went fast, real fast, 'til Aunt Fred looked like a
blob of paint whirling around.

"Having fun?" cried Aunt Fred.

"You bet!" I shouted.

That was only part of the day. Aunt Fred and I
went to a movie, rowed on the lake, then had dinner
at a strange but wonderful restaurant. It had a huge
dance floor and Aunt Fred taught me to tango.

It was way past my bedtime when we got back to Aunt Fred's house.

I had just stumbled into bed when Aunt Fred came in with a mug in her hand.

"Here's a little bed-time drink."

"What is it?" I said.

"Oh, just my secret brew," she smiled.

My eyes opened wide. "This is really it," I thought. " A witch potion!" With all the fun I'd been having I'd almost forgotten Aunt Fred was a witch. And I'd left my garlic necklace on the dresser.

"Drink up," said Aunt Fred.

I decided I'd try it, even if it was a witch potion. I took a tiny sip. It was so delicious I gulped it all down.

"I don't care if you are a witch," I said, smiling at Aunt Fred. "I like you anyway."

Aunt Fred stared. "A witch! Did you say a witch?"

"Oh, oh," I thought. "Now I've got her mad."

But she just threw back her head and laughed.

"So that's what the garlic was about! Oh, Leila, I'm sorry, but it's so funny. Anyway, garlic is supposed to ward off vampires and werewolves, not witches."

I scowled at Aunt Fred. I'd worn that smelly necklace all day for nothing.

"Well Jeremy said you're a witch," I yelled. "He said you work magic so you've got to be a witch."

Aunt Fred stopped laughing and wiped her eyes. "Oh, Leila, the only person I've got to be is me, just me."

I swallowed hard. "You mean you're not a witch? Not even a little bit?"

"What do you think, Leila?" Aunt Fred smiled.

I sighed. I already knew. "I guess Jeremy thinks you're a witch because you're so different. He's probably never met a grown-up like you before. But he's right about one thing." I threw my arms around Aunt Fred. "You really do make magic."

Aunt Fred laughed and hugged me tight, "Oh I knew you'd understand, Leila, I just knew it. I get so tired of people telling me to act my age, don't you?"

I knew exactly what she meant but I'd never thought grown-ups had that problem. And I couldn't imagine why anyone would want Aunt Fred to change one bit.

As I snuggled down under the covers Aunt Fred asked, "What d'you want to do tomorrow, Leila?"

I thought about it. Then I scrunched up my eyes and grabbed her arm. "Aunt Fred! How would you like to zoom into the sky and fly with the wind?"

Aunt Fred grinned. "Leila, I don't have a broomstick, honest!"

"I know that Aunt Fred. But have you ever been up in a hot air balloon?"